O Christmas Tree

Written by Sally Gilmore
Illustrated by Julie Downing

7373 North Cicero Avenue
Lincolnwood, Illinois 60712

Ground Floor, 59 Gloucester Place
London W1U 8JJ

www.pilbooks.com

Permission is never granted for commercial purposes.

Customer Service: 1-800-595-8484 or customer_service@pilbooks.com

Manufactured in China.
ISBN-10: 0-7853-1885-2
ISBN-13: 978-0-7853-1885-9

*W*inter was the best time of year in Blizzard Woods. The sun was shining and the snow was crunchy underfoot. The animals played together on the frozen pond.

"This is fun!" said Fawn. It was her first winter ever.

Suddenly, the animals heard a noise. They scampered to the clearing to see what it was. There, they saw some people cutting down a fir tree. When the tree toppled over, the people carried it away, laughing and singing as they walked.

"Let's follow them," Rabbit whispered to the other animals.

The animals gathered their courage and followed the people to their house. They crept up to a window and peeked inside. They saw that the fir tree was standing upright again. But now it glowed with colorful lights and twinkling decorations. The animals watched the biggest person lift the smallest person high into the air to place a shining star on the tippy-top of the tree.

"It is beautiful," said Fawn.

"I'd like to decorate a Christmas tree, too," Fawn told the other animals once they were back in Blizzard Woods. "But what would we use?"

"Well, we have berries and vines," said Wolf.

"And nuts of all kinds," said Bear.

"There are lots of beautiful things to be found in Blizzard Woods," said Rabbit.

"But first we need the perfect tree," said Fawn.

"How about this one?" Loon asked.

"That is the perfect Christmas tree," Fawn said. All of the animals agreed.

Now it was time to look for decorations to make their perfect fir tree into an actual-factual Christmas tree.

Bear found some acorns in a hollow tree.

Squirrel found a pretty sprig of holly.

Rabbit and Wolf spotted mistletoe high in a tree. They jumped and jumped. Finally, Rabbit was able to grab it.

Loon found some pinecones, which he thought looked very nice.

At last, the animals of Blizzard Woods were ready to decorate their Christmas tree. Their happy voices rang through the frosty forest like merry Christmas music. Paws helped paws twine vines. Birds placed berries on high branches.

The animals had never had such fun!

When the final pinecone was placed on the last fir bough, the animals stood back to admire their Christmas tree.

"It is lovely," said Bear.

"It is the best," said Wolf.

"Something is missing," said Moose.

"Our tree needs a shining star," said Fawn.

"Look," said Owl.

"A star!" Fawn cried.

Indeed, as night fell, a single shining star had risen high in the sky and seemed to settle at the tippy-top of the Christmas tree.

"Our Christmas tree is perfect, at last," said Fawn. "Merry Christmas!"

O Christmas tree, O Christmas tree,
Thy leaves are so unchanging.
O Christmas tree, O Christmas tree,
Thy leaves are so unchanging.
Not only green when summer's here,
But also when 'tis cold and drear.
O Christmas tree, O Christmas tree,
Thy leaves are so unchanging.